A Perfect Day

ALL ABOUT THE FIVE SENSES

Written by Kirsten Hall

Illustrated by Bev Luedecke

children's press®

A Division of Scholastic Inc.
New York Toronto London Auckland Sydney
Mexico City New Delhi Hong Kong
Danbury, Connecticut

About the Author

Kirsten Hall, formerly an early-childhood teacher,
is a children's book editor in New York City. She has been
writing books for children since she was thirteen years old
and now has over sixty titles in print.

About the Illustrator

Bev Luedecke enjoys life and nature in Colorado.
Her sparkling personality and artistic flair are reflected in her
creation of Beastieville, a world filled with lovable Beasties
that are sure to delight children of all ages.

Library of Congress Cataloging-in-Publication Data

Hall, Kirsten.
 A perfect day : all about the five senses / written by Kirsten Hall ; illustrated by Bev Luedecke.
  p. cm. — (Beastieville)
 Summary: When the rain ends, the Beasties run outside and use all five of their senses to enjoy the perfect day.
 ISBN 0-516-24437-X (lib. bdg.)   0-516-25521-5 (pbk.)
 [1. Senses and sensation—Fiction. 2. Stories in rhyme.] I. Luedecke, Bev, ill. II. Title.
 PZ8.3.H146Per 2004
 [E]—dc22
                              2004000118

3 1984 00222 2634

1 2 3 4 5 6 7 8 9 10 R 13 12 11 10 09 08 07 06 05 04

A NOTE TO PARENTS AND TEACHERS

Welcome to the world of the Beasties, where learning is FUN. In each of the charming stories in this series, the Beasties deal with character traits that every child can identify with. Each story reinforces appropriate concept skills for kindergartners and first graders, while simultaneously encouraging problem-solving skills. Following are just a few of the ways that you can help children get the most from this delightful series.

Stories to be read and enjoyed

Encourage children to read the stories aloud. The rhyming verses make them fun to read. Then ask them to think about alternate solutions to some of the problems that the Beasties have faced or to imagine alternative endings. Invite children to think about what they would have done if they were in the story and to recall similar things that have happened to them.

Activities reinforce the learning experience

The activities at the end of the books offer a way for children to put their new skills to work. They complement the story and are designed to help children develop specific skills and build confidence. Use these activities to reinforce skills. But don't stop there. Encourage children to find ways to build on these skills during the course of the day.

Learning opportunities are everywhere

Use this book as a starting point for talking about how we use reading skills or math or social studies concepts in everyday life. When we search for a phone number in the telephone book and scan names in alphabetical order or check a list, we are using reading skills. When we keep score at a baseball game or divide a class into even-numbered teams, we are using math.

The more you can help children see that the skills they are learning in school really do have a place in everyday life, the more they will think of learning as something that is part of their lives, not as a chore to be borne. Plus you will be sending the important message that learning is fun.

Madeline Boskey Olsen, Ph.D.
Developmental Psychologist

Bee-Bop

Puddles

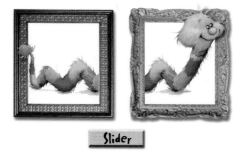

Slider

Wilbur

Pip & Zip

Flippet

Pooky

Mr. Rigby

We're the Beasties

Smudge

Toggles

Zip is looking out his window.
He is sad. He cannot run.

"Pip, we cannot play outside.
Rainy weather is no fun!"

Zip and Pip just have to wait.
They play games and read a book.

Zip looks up and starts to smile.
"The sun is out. Come, Pip. Look!"

"Look! The sun is shining brightly."
They see Smudge is right outside.

Smudge is happy. He is playing.
Birds are playing by his side.

"Listen to the birds!" Smudge tells them.
"They are singing just for me!"

All the birds are singing sweetly.
More birds fly down from a tree.

Toggles walks up with a blanket.
It is big and it is gray.

"Would you like to feel my blanket?"
"It is very soft!" they say.

Puddles runs up. She is smiling.
"These were right outside my door!"

She is holding pretty flowers.
"Come with me! There are some more!"

Puddles shows her friends the flowers.
"Can you smell this bright red rose?"

Smudge tells Puddles, "Let me smell it!"
He sniffs it with his great big nose.

Zip and Pip are picking flowers.
Some are red and some are blue.

Pip picks one and says, "It smells great!
I will give this one to you!"

Slider joins them. Up runs Bee-Bop.
Bee-Bop tells them, "Come with me!

Pooky has some extra berries.
She is waiting by the tree."

Pooky sees her friends are coming.
She stands up and calls out, "Hi!"

"What is that I smell?" asks Slider.
"Did you make a berry pie?"

Smudge can't wait to taste the berries.
"Pooky, this pie is the best!

We should really have a picnic.
We can share it with the rest!"

Everyone is very happy.
They eat pie and then they play.

Zip and Pip smile at each other.
"This has been a perfect day!"

BLUE BIRDS

1. How many birds are sitting on Smudge?

2. How many birds are flying in the air?

3. How many birds are on this page?

SOUNDS LIKE...

"Those" is a word that sounds like "rose." Can you think of any other words that sound like "those"?

A PERFCT DAY

1. Describe your own perfect day. What would happen?

2. How do you feel on days when everything seems perfect?

3. How do you feel on days when things don't go your way?

WORD LIST

a	each	like	red	sweetly
all	eat	listen	rest	taste
and	everyone	look	right	tells
are	extra	looking	rose	that
asks	feel	looks	run	the
at	flowers	make	runs	them
Bee-Bop	fly	me	sad	then
been	for	more	say	there
berries	friends	my	says	these
berry	from	no	see	they
best	fun	nose	sees	this
big	games	one	she	to
birds	give	other	shining	Toggles
blanket	gray	out	shows	tree
blue	great	outside	should	up
book	happy	perfect	side	very
bright	has	picking	singing	wait
brightly	have	picks	Slider	waiting
by	he	picnic	smell	walks
calls	her	pie	smells	we
can	hi	Pip	smile	weather
cannot	his	play	smiling	were
can't	holding	playing	Smudge	what
come	I	Pooky	sniffs	will
coming	is	pretty	soft	window
day	it	Puddles	some	with
did	joins	rainy	sun	would
door	just	read	stands	you
down	let	really	starts	Zip